c.1

JE   Patterson, Lillie
        Jenny, the Halloween spy.
      Drawings by Diane Dawson.   Garrard.
      Illinois c1979.

Jenny, the Halloween Spy

Jenny, the Halloween Spy

By Lillie Patterson

Drawings by Diane Dawson

GARRARD PUBLISHING COMPANY
CHAMPAIGN, ILLINOIS

To
Todd and Traci Houston

Library of Congress Cataloging in Publication Data

Patterson, Lillie
  Jenny, the Halloween spy.

  (First holiday books)
  SUMMARY: Jenny's curiosity leads her into a
world of fairies and elves and on a wild Halloween
ride with the Devil and his headless hounds.
  [1. Halloween—Fiction] I. Dawson, Diane.
II. Title. III. Series.
PZ7.P2768Jan   [E]   78-11538
ISBN 0-8116-7251-4

Jenny, the Halloween Spy

It was Halloween night.
Jenny wondered if the magical beings
might be around.

"I think I will go to town
and do the marketing,"
Jenny said to herself.
Now Jenny was kind,
but she was also very curious.
She did not want
to miss anything
that might be going on.
So this Halloween,
Jenny put on her
hat and coat.
She took her market basket
and started for town.
"I will stop and visit old Nancy,"
Jenny said to herself.
"Some folks say
that Nancy is a witch.

I want to see
what she is doing tonight."
Jenny found the door
at Nancy's house locked.
The curtains were closed.
So Jenny put her ear
close to the door.

She heard
strange sounds inside.
"I wonder what is going on,"
Jenny said.
"I'll peek through the keyhole
and see."
What Jenny saw
made her eyes open wide.

Nancy was by the fireplace.
She said a few strange words
as she took some oil
from a little jar.
Then she touched the oil
to her eyes.
Nancy put the jar
away near the fireplace.

"Something spooky
is going on in there!"
Jenny cried.
"I must find out
what it is about!"
Tat-a-tat-tat!
Jenny knocked on the door.
"It's Jenny, Nancy," she called.
"Let me in."
Nancy unlocked the door.
"How are you, Jenny?"
Nancy said in a friendly way.
"Come in and sit by the fire.
Since this is Halloween,
let's have some cider."
"I'll have a little, thank you,"
Jenny said.

She looked at Nancy closely
and saw that her eyes
were very bright.
"It must be the oil
in her eyes,"
Jenny thought.

Nancy went to get the cider.
As soon as she left,
Jenny hurried to the fireplace.
Quickly, she took out the jar
and touched some oil
to her left eye.

"My goodness!"
she cried in pain.
Her left eye hurt so much
she shut it tight.
Then Jenny moved
to a dark corner of the room.
She did not want
Nancy to see
that her eye was shut.
Nancy came back with the cider.
The two women
drank cider and talked.
After a time,
Nancy went to get more cider.
When she had gone,
Jenny slowly opened
her left eye.

"What do I see?"
she said aloud.
Wee folk
were dancing before the fire.
Others were swinging
from a rafter above.
Some were putting flowers
around the room.

Nancy's small cottage
was being changed
into a grand palace.
The floor
was covered with gold rugs.
Silk curtains
hung from the windows.
The old kitchen chair
had become a golden throne.
Nancy came back
and sat on the throne.
She had a gold crown
on her head.
Jenny was very excited.
The oil
was magical fairy oil.
It let her see wee folk.

The wee folk
were making faces at her.
Something was wrong.
The wee folk did not like
her to spy on them.

Jenny jumped up.

"Good-bye, Nancy.

Thank you for the cider.

I must be on my way."

Jenny ran out of the door.

It shut behind her.
Jenny was frightened,
but she was curious, too.
With her left eye,
she took one last look
through the keyhole.

Sure enough,
there were the dancing fairies
and the beautiful room.
Nancy still sat like a queen
on her golden throne.

Then Jenny closed her left eye
and looked with her right.
She saw only Nancy's kitchen.
Nancy was sitting
on her old wooden chair.
Now Jenny knew for sure
that it was magic oil
in her left eye.

"Strange things
are happening tonight,"
she said.
"I see things
I've never seen before!"
Jenny started on her way to town.
In town, the streets
were filled with people.

Jenny saw many old friends.
She talked first with one,
then with another.
All this time,
she kept seeing wee folk
with her left eye
and friends with her right.
The wee folk
made faces at her.
It frightened Jenny
to spy on them.
She stopped to buy some fruit
at one of the market stands.
She looked down
with her left eye
and saw a wee ugly man
in a ragged suit.

"That wee man
is a pixie,"
she said to herself.
Now Jenny remembered
that these wee men
love to steal things.

They do it for fun
and often give away
what they steal.
However, Jenny forgot
that these wee men
do not like
people to spy on them.
They will play pranks
and lead people astray.
As Jenny watched
with her left eye,
the wee man put some nuts
into his little bag.
"I see you, little man,"
she said.
Without thinking,
Jenny shook a finger at him.

"You should not steal
like that."
The little man
turned around and made a face
at Jenny.
He jumped up and down,
screaming in anger.
"You will never again spy
on fairy folk,"
he shouted.
"The magic oil
will leave your eye."
With these words,
he put his head back
and closed his eyes.
Then he blew at Jenny,
poof!

The little man
blew magic dust
all over Jenny.
"You need a good lesson,"
he said.

"The magic dust
will teach you
not to spy!"
Jenny tried to shake off
the magic dust.

She was very frightened
as she ran toward home.
"If only
I had a horse to ride,"
Jenny thought.
That very minute
an old white horse appeared.
Jenny got on the horse
and took the reins.
"Get up, old fellow!"
she cried.
The old horse
moved a few feet,
then stopped.

"Get up, I said!"
The animal moved slowly
until they came
to an open field.
As they started across it,
Jenny heard the loud barking
of hunting dogs.
The old horse lifted his ears
and started to gallop.
The barking came closer,
and the horse ran faster.
"Stop! Stop!"
Jenny screamed.
But the horse
ran even faster.
She held on
as best she could.

She looked back
to see the dogs.
"Help! Help!"
Jenny screamed.
"Those dogs have no heads!"
On and on
came the headless hounds.
Faster and faster
ran the horse.
Soon Jenny heard
a hunter's horn blow.
"Oh, no!" she cried.
"That must be
the old Devil himself."
The wild chase went on
until the horse
jumped across a pond.

Whoosh!
Jenny fell off
on the far side.
Thump!
She landed on the ground.

Just then
she saw the Devil
jump on the horse
and race away.
The headless hounds
ran behind him
in a cloud of fire.
Jenny jumped up
and began to run.
The wee pixie
was by a tree, laughing.
How he had tricked her!
But Jenny
could not see him.

The magic oil
was gone from her eye.
The Devil was gone too,
for the magic dust
had fallen off her clothes.
"Never again
will I pry and spy,"
said Jenny. She was
a changed person.
Jenny never forgot
that strange Halloween.
She never again
tried to use fairy oil
or spy on fairy folk.